# <u>40 Frightful Flash Fictions</u>

I0534348

## ALLAN M. HELLER

Night to Dawn Magazine & Books LLC
P. O. Box 643
Abington, PA 19001
www.bloodredshadow.com

ISBN: 978-1-937769-40-6
Copyright by Allan M. Heller
Photographer/Illustrator: Stan Horwitz
Calligraphy & design: Teresa Tunaley
Tree photograph by Debra Regis
Editor: Barbara Custer

*To my loving (and lovely) wife, Tatiana, who patiently reads all of my writing (and gives sound editorial advice)!*

*I wish to thank Barbara (of the Balloons) Custer, for her friendship and encouragement, the members of the Hatboro Writers' Group, Ruth Z. Deming and the members of the Coffee House Writers, my in-laws, Martin and Elena Greendlinger; my mother and stepfather, Cynthia and David Jones; my brother and sister-in-law, Laurence and Stacey Heller, and my late father, Stuart H. Heller, whom I miss sorely every day.*

# Table of Contents

# Introduction

Proclaiming that "flash fiction" is the future may be a premature, if alliterative claim. At the same time, denying the huge impact that this diminutive discipline has is inaccurate. Readers will not sit down with *Tom Jones* or *Moby Dick*, and why should they with a myriad other distractions vying for their attention? But fear not! Reading is not defunct, just becoming more compact, generally between 50 to as much as 1,000 words.

Horror, or dark fantasy, is also an attractive venue. People like to be scared, armed with the knowledge that they can always retreat back into the real world, close their eyes, or click their ruby slippers together.

I have sought to combine the public's preference for pithiness with their fancying fear, in this modest 40-tale collection titled, you can guess, *40 Frightful Flash Fictions*. Some stories are supernatural yarns; others cull trepidation from mundane situations. They range in length from the 105-word "The Possession" to the 695-word "Keeping Your Head above Water."

Flash fiction may be a trend, but looks to be a long-lived one. So enter the dark chambers of the imagination, and hang on to every concentrated phrase. You won't want to miss anything.

A.M.H., July13, 2015.
Hatboro, Pennsylvania

# The Tenant from 417

Elmore the janitor found him lying face down in the laundry room, wearing a blue bathrobe and one slipper, the second of which had most likely come off when he slid from the chair by the window and onto the floor. The last person to see Stillman Meckler alive had been Bruce, the hunchbacked octogenarian from apartment 208 who wandered the building after dark like some bored apparition. That was around three o'clock in the morning. Four hours later came the grim discovery.

"A heart attack, I guess," Elmore suggested.

But the tenant from 417, who lived on the same floor as the deceased had, didn't buy it. Why had Stillman locked himself in the laundry room? He intended to find out.

2:57 a.m. He snuck out of his apartment and descended the darkened stairwell, making no sound as he crept down the steel steps. Arriving at the first floor, he delicately shut the door behind him, entered the deserted laundry room, and flicked the light switch. The fluorescent tubes awakened with an angry humming.

He felt a slight chill grip him, as he had dressed the part for added authenticity. Circling the row of washing machines in the middle of the room, he paused by the window where the chair sat. Sensing something, he turned around and saw hunchbacked Bruce walk past. Did that guy ever sleep?

He decided to lock the door, thinking to recreate the mood on that fateful night. The landlord had been very hush-hush about everything, and even the media released no details. Stillman had been depressed. That was no secret. He did have a heart condition and a weight problem. The latter was not surprising, since his neighbors attested that he was constantly buying snacks and sodas from the vending machines in the laundry room. Maybe he had a drug problem, too. He had borrowed money from at least four other tenants. Fred in 418 had loaned him close to a hundred.

A half hour passed, and no revelation arrived. Groggy, he fished in his pocket for change. Four twenties, a ten, and three quarters. With the latter, he bought a Pepsi, which he guzzled in about 90 seconds.

Vertigo rushed through him. The tenant from 417 staggered toward the chair, just managing to sit without falling. Weird thoughts rushed through his mind. He was in high school 30 years ago, and the teacher, Mrs. Keller, was telling the class about Sisyphus, the mythological king who was punished in the afterlife by having to roll a boulder up a huge hill, only to have the rock roll down the opposite slope every time. Forever.

The walls started spinning. His mind succumbed to darkness. Stillman Meckler slid out of the chair and onto the floor of the laundry room.

# The Horse Trader

The murders of a few peasants in Moscow's Shabolovka district was of little concern to the police, who, like most of the Russian populace, were jaded by the violence and anarchy spawned by three successive wars. But after a pattern emerged, authorities were obliged to give the matter some attention. This did not worry the horse trader or his prospective customer, who followed the former back to his stables on a clear fall day in 1921.

"I don't have very much money with me," Alex told the horse trader. "Only three rubles."

"Don't worry, my young *tovarisch*," the horse trader replied. "I think that I have a mare that will be suitable. I'll let you have her for two rubles."

Alex suddenly wondered why the horse trader, a wrinkled, bearded man of about 50, didn't bring the animal to market like the other merchants did.

The horse trader laughed, startling Alex.

"My wife asks me, 'When are you going to get rid of that old nag, Vasya?' And I reply,

'Which one?'" Again he laughed. "But she is a good horse, my friend."

As the two approached the stables, Alex's mind wandered into dark places. The killer's victims, all men and boys thus far, had been discovered on days following the biweekly horse market. Bludgeoned or strangled, the deceased had been bound, placed in burlap sacks, and dumped in the street. The press dubbed the perpetrator "The Wolf of Moscow."

Alex dismissed the misgivings as they both entered the stable, navigating through the thick carpet of straw on the ground. Looking around, Alex saw only one horse, presumably "that old nag."

As Alex studied the mare, Vasili Komaroff, the horse trader, reached into a belt pouch and withdrew a hammer, raising the tool above his head.

"What is your name?" Komaroff asked.

"Alexandra."

Komaroff froze, then lowered the hammer.

"You are a girl!"

Alex turned to face him.

"Yes. My father wanted a son." She shrugged. "I keep my hair very short, like a boy's, to humor Papa."

Komaroff shook his head. "You are dressed like a man, too."

"Safer to look like a man when going to the market alone."

"I don't think I can let this horse go for two rubles, *dyevochka*. I'm sorry."

"As you wish," Alex replied. Then she was gone.

The horse trader wasn't sure whether or not Alex had seen the hammer, but he didn't care. The Wolf knew that he was a monster, but he was not, nor would he ever be, a killer of women.

# The Last Templar

That he and his fellow Templars had attacked a Turkish caravan on the Sabbath did not particularly worry Michel Des Loges. He did not believe that the Truce of God applied to infidels. But the dying words of the caravan master, invoking the wrath of Allah, haunted him.

"Allah is *their* god," Guy Capet sneered. "His Holiness has assured salvation for those who fall in battle against these heathens."

"And Turkish gold is as good as Christian," Jacques Du Bois added, patting his bulging saddlebag.

Des Loges glanced at him disapprovingly. "Greed does not become a knight of the Temple of Solomon."

Du Bois flushed. "Nor does cowardice."

Jerking his horse to a stop, Des Loges dismounted.

Du Bois held up his hand. "Forgive me, brother."

A tense moment passed. The others watched with practiced calm as Des Loges considered the apology, then climbed back atop his steed.

The five rode in silence for an hour, bound for *La Main de Dieu*, a Templar stronghold in Antioch. A glittering in the grass ahead caught their attention. Drawing nearer, they saw the armored bodies of three dozen Turkish soldiers. The stench was unholy.

Claude Racine, one of the younger knights, dismounted and with a spear, started strolling among the corpses, all of whom were in a prostrate position. Weapons still in hand.

"Claude, *attention!*" shouted Leon La Roche, whose black destrier reared up in shock at what occurred next. One of the bodies leapt to its feet, and swinging a battle axe, sliced through Racine's knee. Racine's scream corresponded with La Roche's, as Racine toppled to his side and La Roche over the rear of his horse. Both Templars lay on the ground, one dead and one writhing.

Des Loges, Capet and Du Bois mobilized with the detachment of professional soldiers.

"It is a ruse!" shouted Des Loges, and charged at the infidel, skewering the shoulder of his free arm. Du Bois followed with a blow from his flail that should have snapped the Turk's neck. Yet his foe remained standing. What kind of armor was he wearing?

"Heathen swine!" Capet screamed, striking a blow that his opponent easily parried. Spinning around, the "former corpse" hurled his axe, lodging the blade in the base of Capet's skull. He then reached down, picked up the spear, and punctured Racine's throat.

Des Loges and Du Bois regrouped, and rushed forward for a second assault. Bracing the spear, the Turk skewered Du Bois, and lifting him into the air, tossed him over his shoulder.

But Des Loges was not so easily dispatched. His attack succeeded in severing an arm. Galloping back to deliver the coup de grace, Des Loges saw that the Turk had expropriated Capet's sword. And there was virtually no blood coming from the stump of the missing limb.

With a fierce cry, Des Loges struck again, slashing the enemy across the face, which was concealed by a shroud wrapped around the head and underneath the spiked helmet. This time the Turk fell, but staggered back to his feet.

"Why are you not dead?" Des Loges shouted.

The Turk stepped forward, and with his remaining hand, unwrapped the shroud. Des Loges gasped in horror.

"I am!" a grating voice replied.

The remaining infidels rose to their feet, surrounding and advancing on the last Templar.

# Reflections

A foul odor rather than concern for his health was what led to the discovery of Jerry Pressler's body. When three tenants on his floor complained, superintendent Manny Rodriguez entered the deceased's apartment. The seventy-five-year-old Pressler was supine in the foyer, eyes open, and had a few nicks on his throat, possibly from shaving. In the six months that he had resided at Verdant Vista Apartments, Pressler had managed to offend nearly everyone. There was no autopsy or suspicion; he was bagged and wheeled out on a gurney.

When fifty-two-year-old Sylvia Thompson died in her sleep three weeks later, Rodriguez felt bad, but knew that Thompson had high blood pressure and other health problems. Later that day, Kristen Black, the twenty-something across the hall, told Rodriguez that she had heard someone knocking on Thompson's door that evening, about midnight. That and the scratches on Thompson's throat made Rodriguez wonder.

Desmond Drayton, the security guard who was stationed nightly at the rear entrance, hadn't seen anything strange in his six weeks on the job.

The cameras at the front entrance didn't pick up anything out of the ordinary, either. *The hall cameras*, thought Rodriguez.

The tapes from the night that Pressler died, about three days before he was found, had already been recorded over. Rodriguez entered the office at 11:00 p.m. and scanned the tape from yesterday evening. At 11:47 p.m. Thompson had opened her door and started talking to someone. She then opened it wider and moved aside, as if letting someone in. At 12:31 a.m., the door swung open as if of its own accord, then slowly closed.

There was nobody else on camera.

"What the hell," Rodriguez whispered.

"Close enough," came a voice behind him.

Rodriguez spun the office chair around. Drayton loomed over him.

"How did you get in here?" Rodriguez demanded.

Drayton smiled. "It's not a private residence; it's an office. I don't have to be invited."

Rodriguez paled.

"The tenants are quite trusting, though. When the security guard knocks on their door and tells them it's an emergency, they let him in." He moved closer to the petrified Rodriguez.

"But, but you weren't on the tapes. I watched."

Drayton laughed. "If I don't cast a reflection in a mirror, doesn't it stand to reason that I wouldn't leave an image on camera?"

# Wedded Bliss

Jack and Rhonda Davies hated each other. They stayed together because after five decades, neither had anywhere to go. Jack blamed his three heart attacks on Rhonda, insisting that he'd never been sick before he married her, while Rhonda attributed their son Josh's first and final heart attack to Jack's bad genes.

"You killed my boy," Rhonda would remind him.

"You're killing me," was Jack's retort.

Jack stared at the remains of his grapefruit while stirring his coffee counterclockwise. Rhonda nibbled an English muffin with jam. A steaming cup of Chamomile sat neatly on a saucer. This morning was like any other. Except that it was their 51$^{st}$ anniversary.

"Do you know what today is?" Rhonda asked.

Jack was surprised. Their meals rarely included a helping of conversation.

"Sunday," he replied. He sipped his coffee.

"It's our anniversary."

"So what?" Another sip of coffee.

Rhonda shook her head. "You know that story about Winston Churchill and Lady Nancy Astor? She tells Churchill, 'If you were my husband, I'd poison your tea,' and he replies, 'If I were your husband, I'd drink it.'"

"Everybody knows that story." A generous gulp of joe. "You probably know some kinda drug or untraceable poison. Being a retired nurse."

Rhonda smiled at her husband for the first time in years.

"You're right, darling. I do."

Jack clutched his chest.

# Fortune Cookie Messages

With a smile that dripped saccharin the waitress set the check on the table. Wrapped in cellophane was a stale orange-brown fortune cookie. Opening his modest dessert, Warnick Williams delicately bit the cookie in half, and extracted the thin strip of paper with his thumb and forefinger. Taking off his glasses to read the tiny print, Williams recoiled.

You must leave quickly.

He flagged down a busboy. "Is this some kind of a joke?"

The lanky 15 year-old examined the piece of paper. "It's a fortune cookie message."

Williams snatched the tiny strip.

Rekindle old friendships. Someone who was close to you awaits your call.

The busboy shrugged and proceeded to the kitchen.

Williams was baffled. Looking around him, he saw that he was the only customer left, and that the OPEN sign had been flipped to the opposite message. Maybe they wanted him to go home, and instead of telling him that they were closing, decided to play some elaborate hoax. Eating half the cookie, Williams looked at the miniature message again.

Get out while you still can.

Williams saw his waitress, a short, plain-faced woman with bangs.

"Is it such a problem if I finish my tea?"

She stopped. "No, no problem. Why do you ask?"

"Read this," Williams demanded.

She did. "Rekindle old friendships ..."

"What? Give me that."

Williams read the identical message.

"What the hell is going on?" he asked.

"I don't know, sir. Why are you so angry?"

"Nothing. I mean, I don't know," Williams stammered. "I'll be outta here in ten minutes."

"Okay." She, too, disappeared into the kitchen.

*I must be seeing things*, he thought. Was he allergic to MSG? Funny how before anyone heard of MSG, nobody was bothered by it. What were the symptoms? Headache? Flushing sensation? Diarrhea?

Hallucinations?

But Chinese restaurants didn't use MSG anymore.

He popped the rest of the fortune cookie

into his mouth. With a shaky hand, he picked up the morphing message again.

You were warned.

\*\*\*\*

The explosion that ripped through half a block of Main Street at 9:30 p.m. was likely caused by a gas leak, the Fowlersville Forager reported. Because most of the nearby businesses were closed, the death toll was limited to a patron and three employees of a local restaurant.

# Which is Witch?

The accused were two girls, ages 14 and 16, and a man of 70. They stood trembling before the magistrate who, with his long black robe and severe countenance, looked more frightening than any demon that the alleged witches might have conjured. A fierce-faced woman with long red hair and angry gray eyes pointed a bony finger at the trio as she listed their various "offenses."

"Innocence Mallory cursed my livestock," she hissed, indicating the younger of the two females. "I saw her and Hope Hallowell there next to her, floating across my property last Tuesday. On Wednesday two of my cows died."

She turned her hateful gaze on the old man.

"And Aloysius Brown came to me in a dream, drunk with the blood of infants, and praising the name of The Evil One!"

Fenton Malone, the magistrate, silenced the ensuing clamor with a thump of his gavel.

"You have all heard the charges against you. What say you to these grave accusations?"

The terrified babbling barely coalesced into coherent claims of innocence.

"She is a liar!" shrieked the Hallowell girl. "*She* is a witch!"

"I believe otherwise," Malone replied. "I find you all, Innocence Mallory, Hope Hallowell and Aloysius Brown, guilty of witchcraft, and hereby sentence you to hang on the morrow." A final thump.

When the small courtroom had been cleared and the pandemonium had subsided, Malone asked the bailiff what he thought of the proceedings.

"Disturbing," Tom Bower replied. "I wonder how many others are in league with the Devil. And lie about it."

"On the contrary," Malone said. "Young Goody Hallowell spoke the truth. And Elizabeth Planter *is* a witch."

Bower was incredulous. "Then why did you not acquit the three defendants and arrest the old hag?"

Malone rose with a flourish, spreading his robed arms like the wings of a giant vulture. "Because," he said. "She is in my coven."

# Safety First

To say that Brad McGinnis was unshaken by the death of fellow student Siloam Jenkins would have been unfair. But Brad claimed that the other "safety" on duty, Mary Tipple, was responsible for watching the intersection where the accident occurred. Brad took his yellow sash seriously, and if he saw a classmate jaywalking or crossing on red, he would report the infraction to the principal, Mrs. Malcolm. Mary should have been more observant that September day when Siloam sauntered into the middle of the street and in front of the new Ford Pinto traveling on Mary's side of the road.

Two weeks into October, Brad manned his post at Jefferson and Flanders streets as the hordes of eager kids fanned out in all directions, bound for home. Fewer than half of the students caught the bus to school; most lived within walking distance. After ten minutes Brad spotted a perpetrator. Because of the distance he wasn't sure who the offender was, but the maroon jacket and brown corduroys suggested Patrick Hoyle. Brad began pursuit when someone grabbed him by the collar.

Clem Bagley. Meanest kid in the fifth grade.

Clem scowled. "You're a lousy rat."

Brad swallowed hard. "Clem, I'm just doing my job."

"How much they pay you?"

"N-nothing," Brad admitted. "I'm basically a volunteer student crossing guard."

"Then if you don't get paid, it ain't a job." Clem shoved him. "You ever report me to Mrs. Malcolm, I'll kill you."

Relieved, Brad watched as his tormentor turned and departed. Patrick Hoyle! He was getting away! Glancing left and right, Brad hustled across Jefferson Street, picking up the pace to a jog when he reached the opposite sidewalk. Pat was just a dark red spot in the distance. A rumble of thunder sounded, and the skies instantly darkened. He had to catch up with Pat before the storm started. The rule was that when a safety wrote you up, he had to tell you.

Panting after the first block, Brad kept focused on the figure ahead. The jacket wasn't really maroon or red, but more of a brown color. Pat slowed to a lazy shuffle, then stopped.

Brad walked the last few yards, breathing heavily. He whipped out his pen and notepad. Tiny spatters of precipitation dotted his clothes. The scurrying crowds of students had dispersed.

"Hey," Brad announced. "You crossed on a red light."

As the figure turned to face him, Brad nearly fainted. It wasn't Patrick Hoyle.

"I just wanted to see who was watching this time."

Then Brad was alone, shivering, and staring at the raindrops pounding the concrete.

# The Mortician's Assistant

"You don't mind the graveyard shift, do you?"

The question was posed seriously, but had the unintended consequence of evoking laughter from the mortician and his prospective employee.

Clearing his throat, Reggie Morris continued.

"Really, though. I'm pretty busy here, so I need to know."

Wrigley Saunders, the applicant, assured him that late hours posed no problem, and in fact, were preferable.

"Then I believe we have a match. When can you start?"

Saunders beamed. "Tonight."

The other workers at Morris Funeral Home took an instant disliking to Saunders. He was impatient, rude, condescending, and as one of the chauffeurs put it, "downright weird." When Saunders screamed at Bruce, the driver, for knocking on the door when he was about to begin cadaver preparation, Morris decided to have a chat with his new hire.

Morris arrived at his place of business at

just past midnight on a chilly Wednesday. Bruce was sitting in the office, reading the newspaper, waiting for the next call. The county morgue just brought in a young woman who had been in a horrific head-on collision. After a brief investigation, the accident was attributed to icy roads.

"Lemme tell you, Reggie, this is one of the messiest I've ever seen," Bruce said. "It's a good thing she had ID on her. Closed casket for sure."

Morris nodded. "Where's Wrigley?"

Bruce snorted. "Dr. Frankenstein's prepping the deceased."

Proceeding down the hallway, Morris descended a set of stairs and stopped at a beige door with a numeral three. Strange gurgling sounds made him pause, then knock three times.

"Go away!" a voice from the other side boomed.

Trying the door, Morris found it locked. He fished his keys out of his trouser pocket and jammed the right one into the lock. Maybe Saunders thought that he could talk to Bruce like that.

The door swung open. Saunders crouched naked over mangled human remains on the steel prep table. But he was different. Pale yellow skin, black hair tangled wildly, fingertips tapered into two-inch talons. Blood smeared across his chin and lips. With eyes like gaping wounds, Saunders glared at his boss.

Morris was aghast. Saunders was a ghoul.

# As Clear As Daylight

Orvus Pritchard, Esquire saw Sallie Franklin sitting in the swivel chair behind his antique mahogany desk. She was facing him as he unlocked the door to his office. An attractive, light-skinned black woman in her late thirties, Franklin wore the same white dress that she did that fateful night six months ago. She almost looked normal save for the horizontal slash across her throat. And the bloodstains on her clothing.

Pritchard froze. A weak gurgle emanated from his vocal chords. "No! No!"

Franklin smiled. "What's the matter, Orvus?" She couldn't resist adding, "You look like you've seen a ghost."

"Wh-what do you want?"

"Justice!" she hissed. "I want Phaeton in jail."

"There's nothing I can do!" Pritchard insisted. "Your husband was found not guilty!"

"He lied on the stand! And you know it."

She was right. Phaeton had decided to testify on his own behalf, claiming that he had been out of town on the night of the crime, and hadn't re-

27

turned 'til the following morning. In fact, he admitted to Pritchard that he was home during the time frame in question.

Franklin started flickering like a fluorescent tube about to burn out.

"Tell them he lied. Tell them you knew. Or I'll be back." She vanished.

Trembling, Pritchard took a deep breath, telling himself out loud that he had been hallucinating. As if in response, a leaded crystal paperweight on his desk launched itself against the window, shattering the pane. Pritchard shrieked.

Reluctantly, Pritchard made several telephone calls the next morning. Within days, Phaeton Franklin was in custody and Pritchard was facing disbarment.

Choosing to immerse himself in his threadbare career, Pritchard returned to his office, where he spent 12 to15 hours daily. His wife had barely spoken to him since his dire admission, and his teenage son was making thinly veiled remarks about his father's transgression. As he began dozing off at his desk, he remembered a quote from an old Chinese film, with subtitles, that he had seen as a law school student: *The dead won't harm you. You need only to fear the living.* He didn't hear the telephone ring, or the message informing him that Phaeton had made bail.

****

The spirit haunting the law office believed that taking the form of Sallie Franklin would be most effective. Though he was certain that Pritchard never knew what hit him, this was not the desired outcome. Phaeton Franklin would go to prison and Pritchard ... wherever. The spirit had done many times what Pritchard had done but once. Both he and Pritchard had died at the same desk: he with a brain aneurysm and Pritchard with a bullet in the temple. Redemption was yet to come.

# Red Sky at Morning

The monarch's letter to "Smiling Smedley" Simpson gave *The Chimera* leave to rob those who flew the flag of England's enemies. The crew of the French vessel *Le Ciel Rouge* had fought to the last man, taking 12 of Smedley's privateers with them. Also, the rival ship had sunk during the battle, precluding its capture. That was the start of the bad luck.

Two brutal deaths the following evening troubled Captain Simpson even more. Midshipman Passidus Grimes had been torn to pieces, his remains strewn over the deck. Quartermaster Caspar Barr's neck was broken inexplicably. The murders yielded few clues, with the exception of one astronomical phenomenon. The moon was full. Three of the remaining five men, George Bland, John O'Reilly and Rand Miller, had been with Simpson for over a year. Gustavus Clinton and Mercury Coyne had joined up six weeks ago. All of them were killers; Simpson had no use for altar boys. But was one of them something worse? Simpson assembled his skeleton crew on *The Chi-*

*mera's* deck.

"This night, no one sleeps," he informed the doughty seamen. Patting the flintlock tucked into his belt, he added, "Keep armed and alert. Fate willing, we'll reach port in three days."

A quarter hour past sundown, all was quiet. The sea was still. The moon was full.

A roar shook the deck. Four heads turned and looked at Mercury Coyne. His hands and fingers elongated grotesquely, sprouting coarse brown hair and sharp claws. His lower jaw jutted out as thick fur coated his distorted face. His eyes burned deep crimson. Baring fresh fangs, he cast a fearsome glance at his mates, then bolted toward the main mast, and with uncanny speed, ascended to the crow's nest.

A shot from Simpson's firearm pursued the fleeing fiend, missing by an inch.

"Go up there and get him!" Simpson barked to no one in particular.

After a brief hesitation, George Bland started climbing, his sheathed cutlass at his side. As he neared the summit, a claw swipe obliterated half his face, sending him plummeting to his death. With a triumphant howl, the creature perched on the edge of the basket, then leapt toward the terrified crew. He landed on Rand Miller, dispatching him with a flurry of claw strokes. Both Gustavus Clinton and John O'Reilly drew their sabers, but the beast finished them off with the same deadly alacrity.

Simpson pointed his flintlock at the thing that had been Mercury Coyne, and got off a round before his adversary playfully knocked the weapon from the captain's hand. The monster grinned, advancing slowly on his former commander. Simpson turned and ran towards the starboard side of the ship, climbing over the edge and jumping into the water below.

"I'll drown before I'll let you take me!"

With a snarl, his lupine pursuer followed suit, making a huge splash as he landed a few yards from the captain. When he surfaced seconds later, he was Mercury Coyne again.

"You're a werewolf!" Simpson croaked.

"A shapeshifter," Coyne replied. "And don't worry, Captain. I won't let you drown."

He submerged again, leaving a stream of bubbles in his wake. A full minute passed, and Simpson thought that perhaps Coyne himself had drowned.

Then he saw the dorsal fin cutting through the brackish sea water.

# As One That on a Lonesome Road

Between the suburbs of Wyncote and Elkins Park in southeastern Pennsylvania is a buffer zone devoid of any traffic signals or streetlights. A three-quarter mile stretch of road sneaks between a wooded slope on either side, one of which nestles a shallow creek that rises in and out of existence, depending on precipitation. One summer night many years ago I walked that deserted stretch when my Buick Century T Type broke down.

Of course I was nervous, either that I might get hit by a car, mugged, or even worse. No, the neighborhood wasn't dangerous but people were after me. Bad people. I seemed to be a target for bullies when I was a kid and I had a bad feeling about tonight.

I was about halfway through the aptly-named Forest Hills Drive when I happened to turn around, and saw a person approaching, maybe 60 yards away. He had a small flashlight which he shone on the ground in front of him. He started walking faster, and so did I. Probably I could've outrun him with that much of a head start, but I didn't want to chance his being close enough to find out which street I lived on: Acorn Avenue, just two blocks from where Forest Hills emerged onto Evermore Street. So I stopped and ducked back into the woods about 15 feet. I picked up a tree branch as a precaution. He kept coming.

I tried to be really quiet when he approached, but he turned his head and saw me. I wouldn't have done anything if he hadn't said, "Gotcha!" when he looked at me. But he said it, or something like it, I'm sure. Then I whacked him on the side of the head with the tree branch. He yelled once and rolled a few feet down the hill.

I was scared half to death, but out of danger. He would wake up with a nasty headache, and maybe enough sense to know better than to stalk strangers in the middle of the night. I made it home safely.

Years later I was able to appreciate how lucky I had been. I read or heard somewhere that there had been a murder on that lonesome road. Found the body partially submerged in the creek. Whatever the poor bastard was doing there I'll never know.

# Fly by Night

They expected a crew laden with all sorts of fancy equipment for detecting and identifying spirits. Instead one man arrived, dressed casually, and without a single ghost-finding gadget. He introduced himself as Levi Prisit. Kaye and Kevin Starrett asked him where all his stuff was, but Prisit insisted that he relied on experience and intuition.

Kaye and Prisit sat at the kitchen table while Kevin brewed three cups of coffee.

Prisit folded his hands in front of him. "What makes you think that you have a manifestation?"

Serving the coffee, Kevin joined his wife and Prisit. He described the eerie, high-pitched shrieks at night, the indistinct shapes that appeared and as quickly vanished, and most frightening, the whispered threats.

Prisit leaned forward. "What kinds of threats?"

"I'll kill you both," Kaye said. "You'll never get rid of me. That sorta stuff."

Prisit asked the couple if anything strange had preceded the evening episodes, which began three weeks ago. Thinking a minute, Kevin remembered a dream in which he was lifted out of his body and saw himself and his wife lying in bed asleep. Then, he recalled, he floated upward for about ten minutes, caught in a vortex of black void and hissing sounds. He awoke with a start.

"That was no dream, Mr. Starrett," Prisit said. "You had an out-of-body experience. Astral projection."

"I don't believe in that."

"But you have no trouble believing that your house is haunted?"

Kevin considered the question. "So what does all this mean?"

"Astral travel can be risky, whether voluntary or involuntary. All kinds of ... entities roam the astral plane, some of them malevolent. Sometimes they latch onto unsuspecting travelers. I think one of them latched onto you."

"So what can we do?" Kaye asked.

"You won't like it," Prisit warned. But the Starretts insisted on knowing.

"Offer it a sacrifice. Not human, of course. Maybe a stray dog or cat. Or a pig."

The Starretts were horrified. But Prisit was firm. He suggested perhaps a chicken or a rat instead.

Finally their visitor departed, refusing any money for the "consultation." Kevin raced to the nearest pet store, buying a white rat. Wearing leather gloves, Kevin held the squirming rodent in the kitchen sink with one hand while dispatching the animal with a paring knife. The process was neither quick nor painless. Kevin vomited.

Early that evening, Dalko McFerrin from Spirit Seekers called. Kevin explained what had transpired.

There was no response.

"Hello?" Kevin said.

"You shouldn't have done that," he told Kevin. "First, a sacrifice makes the spirit stronger."

"And?"

A long pause.

"We don't have any Levi Prisit working for us."

# The Holdup

Orion Fulmore had a lot of nerve robbing the same convenience store that he hit a week ago. But he needed another fix. Despite the CLOSED sign, the door was unlocked. The cashier at Mike's Mini-Mart was behind the counter, his back to Fulmore, filling the cigarette pack dispenser. Brandishing a .22, Fulmore ordered him to turn around slowly and empty the register. The cashier didn't move.

Fulmore exploded. "Don't play games with me, man! I'll shoot your ass!"

The cashier replied, "It's hardly worth it. Don't you remember?"

Fulmore had a flashback. He had been high on crack last week. The guy on duty had also been Pakistani; hell, all of them were in these places. Fulmore recalled handing him a paper bag and telling him to fill it. Thirty lousy bucks. The guy tried to explain that most of the money was in the drop safe, and only the manager could open it. Fulmore didn't want to hear it.

"I know you," Fulmore said.

"And I know you," the cashier replied. "I'll never forget you."

"How's that?"

The cashier turned around, revealing a white shirt marred by three bloody holes.

"You were the last thing I saw."

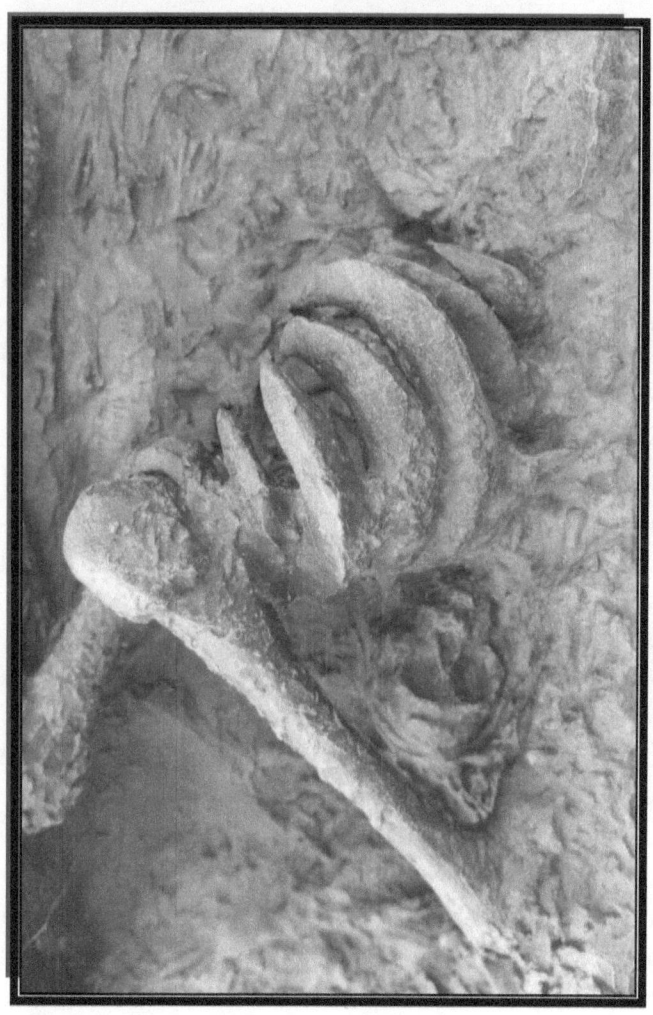

# The Recliner That Ate Mrs. Mulligan

Children's imaginations are very powerful, much more than those of grown-ups, who lose the ability to believe when they get older. To kids, anything is possible. Too bad for adults. And too bad for Mrs. Mulligan, the babysitter.

Lucy Carver hated Mrs. Mulligan, who made Lucy go to bed at 7:00 p.m., and scolded her when she got up after having a scary dream. Lucy was six and a half, a big girl, and she didn't need Mrs. Mulligan telling her what to do.

"Go back to bed, young lady," Mrs. Mulligan said, pointing upstairs. "And don't give me that nonsense about snakes in your closet."

Lucy hated Hobart, too. He was Mommy's new friend. She didn't know why Daddy had to leave. Every time that Hobart came over to take Mommy to dinner or see a movie, they called Mrs. Mulligan.

One night after Mrs. Mulligan yelled at Lucy for spilling a glass of water, Lucy screamed, "I hope that chair you're sitting in eats you!" She was referring to the plush blue recliner in which the babysitter was seated while reading the newspaper.

Lucy stormed upstairs and slammed the bedroom door. Mrs. Mulligan was too stunned to respond. Late that night, Lucy had another scary dream, and cautiously peeked out her bedroom, then snuck down the stairs. Stepping into the den, she saw that the recliner was empty, except for a woman's shoe. Mrs. Mulligan's shoe. Even the newspaper was gone. Lucy smiled.

Mommy was shaking when she came home, and called the police. The policeman and police-woman asked Mommy if she had reason to suspect "fall play." The policewoman, who said that her name was Susan, asked Lucy if she saw or heard anything strange or bad. Lucy shook her head.

A month passed. Mommy told Lucy that she would be in the shower, and to only answer the door if it was Hobart. Hobart knocked at 6:45 p.m., when Mommy was in the bedroom, changing. Lucy let him inside, but didn't say hello back to him. He still wasn't her daddy.

Hobart strolled into the den, looking for a place to sit. Lucy had left her dolls on the blue re-cliner. When Hobart headed toward the kitchen, she offered to clear the spot.

"Sit here, Hobart," she said, collecting her toys. "It's real comfy. I'll tell Mommy you're waiting," she added, walking up the stairs.

Hobart smiled at the little girl. Lucy was a sweet kid after all.

# Dr. Drill

It couldn't have been anything but the Deep Brain Stimulation, or DBS, that had left him with this ability. In attempting to alleviate the symptoms of Lance Hartley's Parkinson's Disease, the neurosurgeon had tapped into some uncharted region of his mind.

Hartley was at home in a wheelchair, recuperating from the procedure, when he made the discovery. His wife, Kitty, was visiting a friend, giving him an interim of blessed solitude. Hartley was staring at a crystal vase on a coffee table in the living room when an angry thought blazed through his convalescing brain. The vase slid across the table, tumbling over the edge and landing sideways on the shag carpeting.

"This operation won't cure you," Dr. George Winston had warned him. "But I think there's a good chance that you'll improve significantly." He then described, in graphic detail, how Hartley would be awake, but under local anesthesia of course, when the doctor drilled through his skull and into his thalamus. The surgeon would then install a set of wires leading to a device known as an Implantable Pulse Generator, or IPG, for regulating electrical signals to the brain.

"My team and I will follow up with you to monitor your progress over the next several months," Dr. Winston explained.

That had been a week ago. Still too early to tell whether the operation was a success. But if he could fine-tune this new ... power, he wouldn't need Kitty to be his caretaker anymore. He wouldn't need her, period. He wanted to tie his own shoes again, to brush his teeth independently, and to shave without help. He wanted his bathroom trips to be private affairs.

He was attempting to right the vase when the lock clicked and Kitty entered. She had that familiar sour look.

"What's my favorite vase doing on the floor?" she snapped.

"I didn't touch your vase."

Naturally, she didn't believe her husband. He was always making messes, of the apartment, of their marriage, of himself. She told him that she sure hoped that this damn "Dr. Drill" knew what he was doing, because she didn't want to take care of a cripple anymore.

Hartley's eyes flashed. "You won't have to."

**\*\*\*\***

"Kitty was very depressed," Hartley explained. "The stress was just too much for her."

He pretended to wipe a tear. Still, the detectives didn't understand how Kitty had managed to hurl herself through the two-inch plate glass window that overlooked John F. Kennedy Boulevard in Center City, Philadelphia. Even if she ran full speed.

# The Protégé

The old man had taken Forrest Woods under his wing a few years ago, had encouraged him, arranged public readings of his work, and introduced Woods to an agent. With over 20 published collections of poetry and dozens of awards, the old man had been a literary dynamo in his day. But at 93, he was past his prime. He hadn't written anything in eight months. Add that to the fact that the old man was a childless widower who lived alone in a three-bedroom house, and Woods had all the incentive he needed.

Gates Bremen frequently nodded off during visits, and Woods used one of these opportunities to smother his mentor. After the deed Woods flushed the latex gloves down the toilet, watching nervously as the murder accessories twirled clockwise into oblivion. He waited 15 minutes, then called 911 and reported that he had just arrived at Bremen's house, found the door open and Bremen unresponsive.

Woods was fond of the old man, but after 21 years, the town of Bilbright, Maine needed a new poet laureate. The position carried a $500 stipend, but Woods was more interested in the fact that Bremen had left everything to him.

An envelope lay on an escritoire, underneath an old fountain pen. Bremen had scribbled something across the front, probably just to test whether the pen still worked. Woods didn't bother examining the envelope or its contents. He didn't believe that Bremen had anything worthwhile to say. Or that the old man was clairvoyant.

### Gates at the Gates

*I must today give Death his due*

*For I was murdered, Woods, by you.*

*In Paradise I'd hoped to see*

*My protégé, but you won't be*

*In any place where angels roam.*

*A fiery pit will be your home.*

*Destroy this note to no avail:*

*I've placed a copy in the mail.*

*G.B.*

# Texting One, Two, Three

Hey, girl! What's up? Pam & me are at that new Mexican restaurant. Free 'ritas w/food. On #4. Think I M drunk. Food ok :)

------------------------------------------------------------

Hey, Margaret! U still w/Ricky? Heard some new guy caught ur eye. Ur not married, why not keep options open? :)

------------------------------------------------------------

Margaret? What's w/formal stuff? Keeping options open but not 4 this guy. Never met him. 1st I thought wrong # but he keeps texting. Weird stuff. Might change my #.

------------------------------------------------------------

He calls from unlisted?

------------------------------------------------------------

Think he uses throwaway cells. How R U?

------------------------------------------------------------

Not great. Wanted to talk 2 U 2 nite, ok, like 10?

------------------------------------------------------------------
------------------------------------------------------------------

Ok w/me but thought you had early meeting 2 morrow 4 work.

------------------------------------------------------------------
------------------------------------------------------------------

They won't fire me if I M a little tired or miss this once.

------------------------------------------------------------------
------------------------------------------------------------------

How can they fire u? Ur the boss!

------------------------------------------------------------------
------------------------------------------------------------------

Just kidding! U at 2911 Union St right?

------------------------------------------------------------------
------------------------------------------------------------------

Who is this? Where is Jen?

------------------------------------------------------------------
------------------------------------------------------------------

Jen can't talk now. Or later. C U soon. Remember to keep ur options open!

# A Keen Acquisition

The Keen Gallery in Los Angeles had a reputation for acquiring items that blurred the line between art and artifact. The 15th-century Samurai sword from the Muromachi Period was a perfect example. Proprietor Evan Barman had purchased the ancient blade, together with its leather-bound scabbard, for $5,000, and was hoping to sell it for twice as much. Kurt Eckert seemed willing to oblige him.

"The owner of this *katana* was killed in a duel, before he even had a chance to draw," Barman explained to a curious Eckert.

"May I take a closer look?"

"Sure."

Barman held the scabbard while Eckert drew the weapon. Gripping the pommel with both hands, Eckert was impressed at the keen edge, which glinted ominously. He playfully moved the sword left and right, up and down, in a forward thrust.

He focused again on the blade, now streaked with red. Blood dripped onto the carpeting of the art gallery. When interrogated by police, Eckert had no recollection of the "brutal crime," and contradictory to what two horrified patrons had sworn, insisted he didn't speak a word of Japanese.

# Joyride

As president of Mythic Motors Corporation, Quince Blayton was accustomed to correspondence chiding his company for irresponsible advertising. But the letter from a grieving mother, citing gross negligence and alluding to a lawsuit, was a first. Blayton didn't think that Mrs. Regina King had a case, but asked his administrative assistant to fire off a professional, yet sympathetic response.

He was driving his own 2015 Tornado LE coupe when a commercial for the vehicle blasted over the radio.

Blayton scoffed. Mythic Motors was no different than any other automaker. If Regina King's son ran into a tree at 65 miles per hour, that was his own fault.

"Stupid kid," Blayton muttered.

The engine roared as Blayton's foot crushed the accelerator. 40. 45. 55. 70. Blayton lifted his foot off the pedal, but the car still raced forward. What the hell was going on? The vehicle was closing in on a pickup truck stopped at a red light. 75. 80. Blayton screamed.

*"Experience the raw power of the car that's taking the automotive world by storm,"* the radio announcer said.

The tires screeched as the Tornado decelerated to 50, shot around the truck, and flew through the intersection. A horn blared. Blayton tried the brakes to no avail as the car zigzagged past a dozen other vehicles. The speedometer read 60.

*"The new 2015 Tornado, from Mythic Motors!"*

The needle hit 72 as the car leapt over a dip in the road, briefly going airborne before landing with a loud bump 20 feet away. Blayton was inches from a heart attack as the psychotic car zoomed toward a railroad crossing just as the semaphore began flashing.

The train's whistle exploded inside Blayton's head as the Tornado snaked through the horizontal barriers, just clearing the 6:15 local. The car whirled counterclockwise for five seconds before coming to rest on the shoulder of the road. Blayton collapsed forward onto the steering wheel, setting off an interminable honking.

*"Take it for a spin!"*

# Flash in the Field

The mutilated earth spat out clumps of soil as artillery shells tore into the French First Line, seven kilometers from Verdun. Corporal Thierry Roget crouched in his trench, the shredded remains of two comrades from his battalion flanking him. Another mortar round exploded five meters away. Cautiously Roget lifted his head, and noticed a French officer—a captain by his insignia—calmly surveying the battlefield. The captain looked at the astonished corporal.

"It's all right," he said to Roget. "Come out of there."

Roget climbed out of the gory pit as the murderous barrage continued around him. The screams of dying men cut through the air. But Roget was not afraid.

"Did Colonel Driant send you to get me?"

The captain shook his head. "Not Colonel Driant."

Roget beamed. "You are my guardian angel! That last artillery shell would have killed me but for you."

"I am not your guardian angel," the captain replied. "That last artillery shell did kill you."

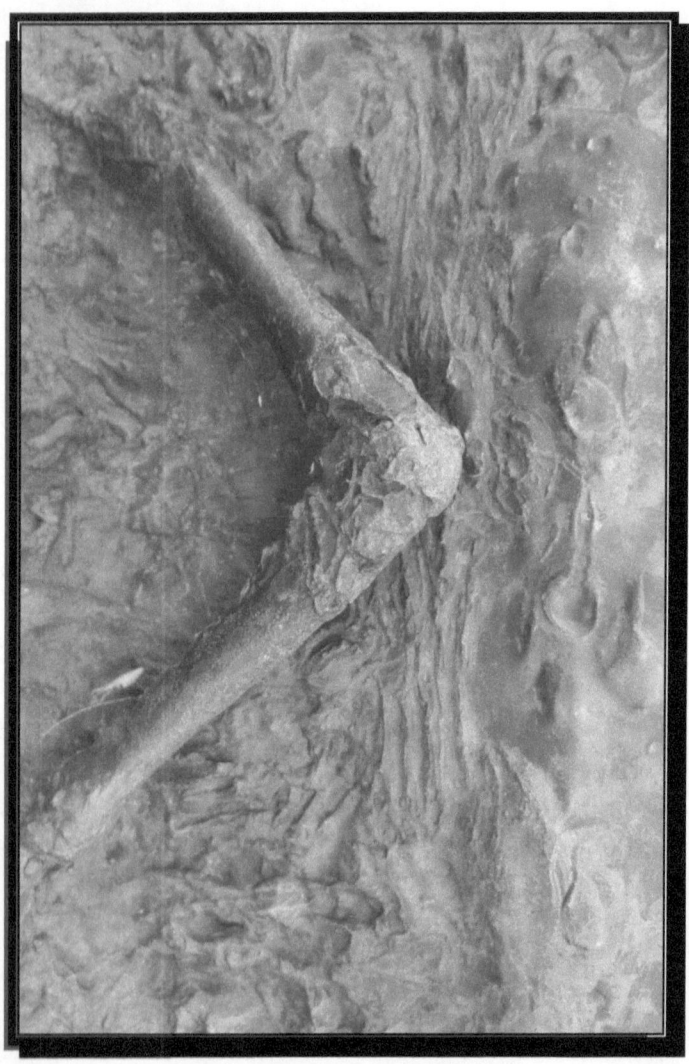

# Automatic Writing

Father Rankin cautioned Alicia Jenkins against engaging in "a pagan, devilish and inane practice," to which she countered that the third adjective rendered the first two invalid. This did not placate Father, so Alicia decided not to bring it up in confession again.

One rainy afternoon Alicia was in her bedroom with a leather-bound notebook, a fountain pen, and a jar of ink on an antique writing desk. She was writing to anyone she thought might answer, the way someone would with a Ouija board, and she felt that these retrograde items lent integrity to the process. Dipping the pen into the ink, Alicia jotted the first line and waited. With whom would she communicate today? Robert Frost? Eleanor Roosevelt? Her own great-great grandmother?

*Tell me something.*

Alicia let her hand rest, holding the pen, which after a minute began to scrawl words.

I was pleased with the offerings. They were wrong in thinking me vengeful. He is vengeful.

Alicia wrote: *Who is vengeful?*

The response ignored the question. Can you help me, kind girl?

*What can I do for you?*

Read!

The pen went out of control, scribbling all over the page, crossing the ruled lines, with loops and swirls. At last the chaos evolved into a type of script which resembled Hebrew or Arabic. Alicia read the message aloud, incredibly understanding every word.

There came a loud thumping, after which the electricity went out. From a column of heat waves materialized a bipedal creature with the head of a calf. Red, muscular limbs sprouted from a stocky frame, from which intense heat exuded. The hideous maws formed what passed for a grin. The creature answered the question that Alicia was too petrified to ask.

"I am Moloch, the 'abomination of the children of Ammon,'" it grated.

Alicia's last thoughts were of Father Rankin.

# Writers, Retreat!

Six hundred dollars to rent a lakeside cabin for one week in the woods of northern Maine. Endowed with a rudimentary beauty on the outside, but with all of the modern amenities within. Not just any writers' retreat, but one that had been owned by the late, great Belton Horst. Horst had been at his most prolific in the two years following his diagnosis with brain cancer, writing three bestsellers. A month after number three, Horst, faced with the reality of his diminishing mental capacity, killed himself á la Hemingway, in the same cozy little lakeside cabin where Crispin Clarkson was now staying.

The locals were a bunch of provincials, Clarkson concluded, especially after the proprietor of Halverson's Deli refused to deliver to the old Horst cabin. Rumors floated that Horst's two-year bonanza was due to a pact with the Devil. When Clarkson responded, "I thought the Devil gave you seven years," the townsfolk were not amused, most refusing to even speak with him again.

Clarkson was there to write, hearsay about demonic deals be damned! He sat at the kitchen table, which provided a splendid view of Lake

Conifer, and set up his laptop.

### Blake's Bluff by Crispin Clarkson

> Henry Blake would get even with Holt Brothers Property & Casualty for denying his claim. Investigators had determined that the accident was Blake's fault, and that while they were very sorry that he was rendered a paraplegic, they were under no obligation to "dispense any compensation." Holt seethed as he …

Clarkson paused. It was six o'clock in the evening. He felt sleepy and decided to retire early.

He awoke at noon the following day. Instead of showering or eating, he returned to his literary endeavors, yet produced nothing. Cursing, he paced around the cabin, tried the front door, and found it stuck.

Deciding that he didn't really want to go out, Clarkson tried to write something again, became discouraged after five minutes, and decided to lie down and wait for inspiration.

"Holt seethed as he. Holt seethed as he thought—no. Holt seethed—damn it!"

Alarmed, Clarkson woke up. It was 3:00 a.m.. He returned to the laptop, staring into its screen.

He typed as he spoke. "… thought about what the rest of his life would be like with…"

Clarkson swore, deleting all but a few words.

### Blake's Bluff by Crispin Clarkson

Henry Blake would get even with Holt Brothers Property & Casualty for denying his claim. Investigators had determined that the accident was Blake's fault,

Two more days passed without a word written, or a bite eaten. Clarkson wasn't hungry. He looked in the mirror. Where was his ... thing for getting rid of whiskers? That thing for ... scraping? No, not scraping. Oh, forget it. He wanted to finish at least the first couple of pages of his ... fiction book. Deciding to start with a clean slate, he faced the laptop again.

### Blake's Bluff by Crispin Clarkson

\*\*\*\*

Sheriff Wilfred Eames was called when Clarkson was found in the woods, a mile from the cabin. Apparently he had smashed the window and crawled out. Clarkson was staring at the trunk of a pine tree, unresponsive when Eames approached him. The doctors at Montgomery Hospital seven miles away determined that the writer was dehydrated, malnourished, and in a catatonic-like state. Subsequent brain scans revealed nothing — absolutely nothing.

# Ghost of a Chance

Paxton Brackley wasn't afraid to die. Caught by London "Killer" Miller, he expected nothing less. Coolly staring down the barrel of Miller's Smith and Wesson, Brackley taunted the bounty hunter.

"Go ahead, do it. I wouldn't waste no time killing you."

Miller had taken down Brackley's horse, leaving the outlaw stranded 15 miles from Tempe. Brackley's gun lay in the sand next to the dead animal.

Miller grinned. "I'm trying to figure out where to shoot you. In the head or in the belly."

Brackley spat defiance. "At least I humped your mama last night."

Livid, Miller replied, "The first one's in your knee!"

Miller aimed, then froze. Fear spread over his face. A man had materialized behind Brackley, his shirt sporting a bullet hole.

"Chance Devereaux?" Miller exclaimed. "You're already dead!"

Miller emptied his gun at the apparition, the shots kicking up clumps of sand.

Brackley reached behind his back, withdrew a concealed derringer and fired. Miller slid out of the saddle.

"So are you."

*Funny how the desert played tricks on you,* Brackley thought.

# Dark Desires

He lay on top of the covers, naked and aroused. In the six months since his wife had left, he had run through the cycle of loss a dozen times, settling for the moment on resignation. Tonight he waited for someone else, calmly exhilarated and fearful at the same time.

He didn't hear her enter; she was just there, a sultry silhouette standing in the doorway. Neither spoke as she strode across the floor, climbed into bed, and straddled him. He guided her with his arms, strong, lonely arms. As he stared up at her, grunting, he discerned an ethereal outline of leathery wings sprouting from her shoulders. Her lips burned bright red as she licked a long tongue over them.

He knew where she came from. He knew and he didn't care.

# Where There's One

The patter of filthy little feet across the attic floorboards alerted Hesh Conklin to the presence of an unwanted visitor. The rat stopped and looked at him, twitching its long white whiskers. Conklin stared back, unflinching, and withdrew a four-inch folding knife that he carried for such occasions. Ample practice on squirrels, birds, and an occasional cat had honed his aim. The rat shrieked once as the airborne blade pinned it to the base of a sloping roof beam.

Retrieving his weapon, Conklin grinned. He scanned the 15'-by-25' room, looking for more quarry. He had already forgotten why he had gone up in the attic in the first place. Hearing a faint sound, Conklin took a step forward. A second rodent darted out of the shadows and stood on its hind legs, observing him.

"You remind me of my ex-wife," he told the intrepid rat.

Conklin raised the knife above his head.

"Stay right there, you little..."

This time it was Conklin who shrieked, as

he stepped into the opening for the pull-down ladder and tumbled to the floor eight feet below. His legs and several ribs broken, he tried dragging his shattered body to the telephone, on an end table across the room. Every inch was agony.

Something dropped onto his back, something light and small with tiny, sharp claws. Then another and another. Rats rained down from the open attic, and began biting him. Their horrid, high-pitched squeals filled his head.

The telephone rang, taunting him.

# Pal's Tickets

Joe Maslin wondered how Pal Lampo became so lucky. The 76-year-old widower defied the basic principles of gambling. Lampo was cashing in the first of 20 winning tickets that he bought an hour before the lottery drawing last night. He'd hit big on 666. Last week, he bought five instant $1 tickets and won $200.

Lampo peeled off a note from the stack of twenties that Raj the cashier handed him and returned it.

Raj nodded. "Thank you, sir."

"I wish I had your tickets," Maslin said. "Most I ever won was $5 on one of them scratch-offs."

The old man smiled. "Be careful what you wish for."

Maslin bought a pack of Marlboros and headed to Greenfingers Tavern. Three hours and nine beers later the bartender flagged him. Maslin didn't remember what time he arrived home, but had a vague recollection of being somewhere that he wasn't supposed to be. Fully dressed, he finally collapsed onto his own bed, which began to spin.

The radio came on at 8:00 a.m., waking him. Something about a burglary. Sitting up quickly, Maslin nearly lost consciousness. A wave of vertigo washed over him. He saw dried blood on his clothes. Reaching into his shirt pocket, he found over a dozen slips of paper. Lottery tickets. Stained with blood. The numerals 666 were visible on the top ticket.

Pounding on the door startled him.

# Hide and Seek

Ronnie explained the game in simple terms to Ted and Zackary: "The person that nobody can find wins." The playing field, Ronnie continued, consisted of their three respective houses, conveniently located in a row along Capitoline Street. Both indoors and outdoors were in bounds.

Zackary was "it" first, and after a two-minute head start, found a place in Ted's bedroom closet. As he entered the two-story house, Ted's parents waved to him from their lawn chairs in the front yard.

The closet was dark, stuffy and packed with shirts and slacks on hangers. A dozen pairs of shoes on the floor made blending in easy. Uncomfortable, but a great hiding spot. Only a thorough inspection would reveal Zackary's presence.

After ten minutes, Zackary began to panic. The sensation that he was not alone dogged him. He remembered tales of the Boogie Man, who lurked under beds and in closets. Feeling something ice-cold squeeze his arm, Zackary almost screamed. But he didn't.

Zackary won hide and seek that day.

# The Assignment

Although he had qualified as an expert marksman in the Russian army, Evgeny Makarov seldom carried a gun, preferring to dispatch his victims with a tremendous bear hug. A former Olympic wrestler and weight lifter, Makarov had 16 assassinations to his credit, three of which were ordered by the Russian president himself. These assignments never came directly from the top, but a second or third-party messenger.

This time Makarov's target was in Saint Petersburg, staying at a hotel on Marat Street. She was a reporter, critical of government policies, and had thus far narrowly avoided arrest by not criticizing the president directly. But that didn't matter.

Makarov shaved his beard, moustache and head the day before his arrival. He donned the uniform of a bellhop.

Locating room 377, Makarov knocked on the door firmly. The bellhop uniform suddenly seemed too small for Makarov's impressive frame, and he felt the tight sleeves press on his arms, and the buttons on his jacket about to pop.

A young woman answered.

"Ekaterina Zarova?"

"Yes?"

"Room service," Makarov said, lunging to embrace her.

His legs stiffened as the tight slacks constricted them. Pain raced up his groin and encircled his buttocks. Makarov nearly fell forward as the jacket squeezed his torso like a ravenous python. The material solidified from cloth to concrete. Makarov's breathing slowed to periodic gasps. The reporter looked on in terror.

Makarov was beet red, his face a balloon about to burst. His eyes bulged. The sound of ribs cracking erupted.

Ekaterina Zarova gagged at the gruesome mess that was her would-be killer. She would have one hell of a story at least.

# Zero at Six O'clock

A dogfight with a determined Japanese A6M had delayed Riordan Manning's return to base in Rangoon. A skilled if somewhat reckless pilot, Manning had outmaneuvered the enemy with a swift dive, arcing around and delivering a stream of 50-caliber bullets from behind. Manning watched with grim satisfaction as the other aircraft descended in a twirl of thick black smoke, igniting into a fireball upon smacking a hillside.

Manning was lucky to still be flying. Two days earlier Base Captain Solon Sanford had ordered Manning to break off pursuit of two fleeing zero fighters. Pretending not to hear his CO, Manning finished off one of the stragglers, but not before his fellow pilot Crewton Laws had been forced to bail out of his crippled plane. He was still missing.

"We need every able-bodied pilot to protect the convoy that's headed down the Burma Road Wednesday," the captain told Manning. "But you pull a stunt like that again and I'll have you court-martialed."

Manning wondered about that. As volunteers for the Chinese Air Force, the Flying Tigers were not officially members of the United States military. Still, he didn't want to push his luck.

His P-40B Tomahawk cruised along at about 300 miles per hour. Another few minutes to landing. Lagging behind his squadron, Manning heard what sounded like the humming of an A6M on his tail.

"Zero at six o'clock!" he barked into the radio. "Zero at six o'clock!"

A crackling response at first, which became Captain Sanford's voice.

"Manning, where are you?"

The vicious report of machine gun fire exploded behind him, ripping holes into his tail. His plane was spewing black smoke. Trying his favorite aerial stunt, Manning executed a sharp dive, but the other pilot kept up, seeming to read his mind. Alarmed, Manning realized that it was not a Japanese A6M, but another P-40B. Noticing the number on the fuselage, Manning nearly fainted. It was 34, Crewton Laws' plane. But that was impossible.

He grabbed the radio receiver. "Captain, it's Laws! He's gone crazy!"

"Is this some kind of a joke, Manning? Return to base immediately. That's an order!"

His plane's left wing sprouted a dozen bullet holes. Looking into the mirror, Manning could see Laws bearing down on him, grinning. Ahead he could also see the landing strip coming into view. Almost home. Another burst of machine gun fire.

Flames in the cockpit. Manning ejected from the plane, which spiraled to a fiery demise. Within minutes of his touching down, a pair of jeeps rushed to greet him. Sanford hopped out of one of them.

"Why did you bail? You wrecked a $40,000 plane!"

"Laws was on my tail!" Manning insisted. "He was trying to kill me!"

"We saw you coming in. There was nobody on your tail."

Manning shook his head. "I saw him. He was after me."

"We found Laws this morning," the captain replied. "His parachute didn't open."

# Folly Fulfilled

The amorphous white form swayed menacingly at the foot of five year-old Eric Massey's bed, extending what passed for arms in an attempt to grab the terrified child.

"I am the Boogie Man," a deep voice groaned.

Eric shrieked. The "phantom" laughed, letting the bed sheet fall to the floor. Eric's 12-year-old brother Wally grinned, pleased with his recurring prank.

Reggie and Marge Massey rushed into their sons' bedroom. Marge flicked the light switch. After calming Eric, the Masseys went back to bed, warning Wally that they would brook no more disruptions.

When the boys were alone again, Wally whispered fiercely, "I am the Boogie Man, Eric. And I'm gonna get you."

****

The following morning was the Masseys' worst nightmare: the window was open and Wally was gone. Eric swore a dozen times that he didn't see or hear his brother leave. Search teams combed the area. An Amber Alert was issued.

Eric lay wide awake in bed that night. When he finally decided to close his eyes, a soft rustling opened them. The sheet had returned, twisting and writhing, but without the verbal taunts. Eric stared with terror at the form, which gradually acquired the faint likeness of a face, Wally's face, puffy and distorted.

"Help me, Eric," the thing croaked. "I don't want to be him!"

"Wally?"

"Help me!" the specter repeated.

The words disintegrated into incoherent babbling, then what sounded like weeping.

"Mom! Dad!" Eric screamed.

# Tiger, Tiger

In his 18 years as head zookeeper, Euclid Crotts had seen the calmest carnivores turn into snarling, ravenous beasts when tossed a slab of fresh meat. He explained this to his new charge, Augustine Rogers. The zoo was closed Sunday, which provided an opportunity for the training.

Crotts was not enthusiastic about having to work with the 19-year-old Rogers, a recovered heroin addict with shifty eyes and an evil scar that traversed his lower lip. His arms were tableaux of tattoos. Who would hire such a lowlife? The zoo, with its new program to help rehabilitate non-violent offenders.

The two men walked by the long rectangular cage that housed Big Bo, the 650-pound Siberian. The cat paced relentlessly, ignoring the pair of puny humans just beyond his reach. The men were in a moat-like structure, five feet wide and four feet deep, which surrounded the tiger pen. A short berm had been constructed to keep visitors at a safe distance.

Pointing to a panel on the side of the cage, Crotts indicated a vertical slot. Unclipping from his belt a large key ring nearly filled to capacity, he explained, "This green one opens the door on the end, so the staff can get in."

He jingled the bunch for effect, then grabbed a red key. "But first, you gotta bring down the divider in the middle of the cage. As Crotts inserted the red key into the control panel slot, a mini portcullis sealed off half the cage, the half where Bo was. With the green key Crotts opened the cage and entered. The tiger regarded him curiously.

"Get the chow, Rogers," Crotts shouted, at which Rogers skewered a 12-pound hunk of venison lying in a metal wagon, and hurled the bloody mass into the cage. Bo growled, his yellow eyes narrowing to slits.

Rogers shut the door, locking Crotts in the cage. The zookeeper looked at him with astonishment.

"What the hell are you doing?"

"Remember when you asked me what my 'specialty' was? Mugging old ladies or robbing banks?"

Crotts paled.

He flashed the encumbered key ring. "Picking pockets."

Rogers inserted the red key into the panel.

# The Possession

The two women hurriedly led Father Bell up the stairs to the little girl's bedroom, where young Meriwether Atkins lay, feverish and breathing faintly.

Father Bell was puzzled. He turned to the child's aunt, Constance Zukerman.

"You told me this was a matter of demonic possession. This child is very ill, but needs a doctor."

The girl moaned.

Charlotte Atkins, the mother, spoke this time.

"We told you the truth," she said. "Meri's fever was caused by wicked spirits, although she herself is not possessed."

"Then who is?"

Aunt and mother turned toward the hapless priest, their faces warped and swollen, their eyes smoldering pits.

# The Caller

She was educated, intelligent and beautiful, not the kind of woman one would expect to take calls from lonely losers on an adult chat line. But she did five afternoons per week, charging three dollars per minute of conversation. Her clients tended toward the masochistic, low self-esteem type, drawn to her suggestive profile photo on the web site, and her tagline: Polly, the loser abuser! Insecure creeps called continuously, earning Ellen Peterson $2,500 to $3,000 dollars weekly. One day, having amassed considerable capital, the Loser Abuser decided to "go legit" and return to real estate, purchasing a luxury apartment building in Miami.

Not all of the losers liked that. Bedford, who had called every day for six months, discovered "Polly's" real name and office number, which he called relentlessly when his emails to www.fleetingflirtations.com were ignored. Peterson had milked Bedford for all he was worth, enticing him to buy her gift cards for high-end boutiques, and furnish her new condominium. He thought he was entitled to a little more attention. She disagreed. Finally, in response to his intrusions, she wrote him a profanity-laced e-mail threatening to expose his peccadilloes to his wife and employer, along with sending several choice photographs he had taken of himself, if he didn't desist. A quiet week passed.

She was driving her Lexus on the highway when the radio went haywire. Adjusting the tuner, she heard Bedford's voice.

"Hello, my goddess. I've missed you."

Peterson trembled so violently that she barely held onto the steering wheel.

"Where are you calling from?" she demanded.

A laugh. "The undiscovered country from whose bourn no traveler returns."

This time she couldn't hold onto the steering wheel. Swerving into the left lane, she hit two vehicles, smashing through the center guardrail before hitting a third car head on. Witnesses heard laughter coming from inside the car, but rescuers later maintained that this was impossible.

# The Reunion

July, 1985. A reunion for alumni of Camp Halcyon. 45 former campers and counselors who were there between 1971 and 1978 descended on the 55-acre site. The get-together was a weekend event, with recreational activities like those back in the day. After a picnic gorge-fest that would give a starving bear an upset stomach, the crew drifted into vacant bunks in the old cabins.

I reminisced about happy times, especially the wonderful, scary campfire tales we shared, like those about Old Man Mooselot. "He went crazy after his wife died," Jared Baker claimed. "He *killed* his wife!" Scotty Dugan said. We had willingly suspended our disbelief about the psychotic, one-armed septuagenarian who lurked in the surrounding woods, armed with a rusty hunting knife. Old Man Mooselot was a legend.

Now attendance was flagging. My beloved summer haven would likely close next season. No more reunions. Camp Halcyon needed something to make it memorable. Fodder for a real campfire tale. I owed it to future generations.

I hadn't notified anyone that I was attending this reunion. Officially, I wasn't there. Making my way over patches of protruding tree roots and slumbering grass, I selected Cabin 3. The knife in my pocket demanded release. They were all asleep. And one of them would never wake up.

Welcome home, Old Man Mooselot.

# Right of Way

Giving the punk in the Camaro the finger was a mistake. Kylie Matthews should have pulled over and let him pass, but his honking and flashing lights made her mad. He had been on her tail a mile before Kylie's imprudent gesture. Now he was chasing her, his profanities audible through closed car windows.

The streets were dark and empty. Kylie had an idea, one whose success depended on Camaro's not knowing the back roads. Her Toyota squealed into a sharp left from Massington Boulevard onto Eames Avenue. Her pursuer barely managed to keep up, which enraged him more.

Kylie counted the seconds as both cars approached 50 on the residential street.

The winter had been brutal, leaving many roads riddled with potholes. Camaro obviously didn't know about the huge crater on Eames, about 30 yards past the lime green house with the birdbath in the front yard.

Kylie swerved. Camaro didn't. He hit the opening hard, shearing off two hubcaps and ripping apart the right front tire.

Relieved, Kylie made the third right onto Belvidere Street, then the second onto Rhodes Lane. She scrambled to beat the traffic light at Massington, but burned the left as the signal flashed from yellow to red.

She flew down Massington, headed for home. A motorcycle tried to ease out from Lexington Lane, but Kylie had no time to let him in. Another horn blared. Then six or seven more. A flood of bright headlights shone from behind her, followed by the cacophonous roar of 10 Harley Davidsons, surmounted by a gang of bikers.

# During the Heat Wave

You won't find no newspaper articles about the heat wave in Clover Corners, Pennsylvania -a small town outside of Pittsburgh- in 1971. Them deaths were officially listed as "mundane" causes—heatstroke, heart attack, a domestic fire, but eyewitnesses knew this wasn't true. Mable McCarthy started sweatin' buckets while she was in line at the post office, then collapsed. Jasper Clevington was walkin' along Brewster Boulevard when he started smokin' - and I don't mean no cigarette. Never screamed—just started shakin' while them white tufts was risin' off him. Then he went down. Pat Horton -the county coroner and a friend of my Pop, said Jasper had third-degree burns. Cuddy Masters had it worst of all; he was in his kitchen fryin' an egg when he got his: wife Athena said he melted—right in front of her eyes!

Everybody who saw them "accidents" said the same: the victims' bodies got blurry, the way things do in summertime when heat rises off of 'em. But this was October.

Now I know what you're thinkin': some

freaky, Halloweeny stuff. But it was the 23rd, 24th and 25th of October. Whatever it was moved like an invisible stalker, and there wasn't no common thread between victims. One was a 69-year-old widow. Jasper was a World War I veteran. Cuddy Masters was a middle-aged machinist; a drunk who slapped Athena a little, but he didn't deserve that.

I heard about "spontaneous combustion," where folks just burst into flames. But there wasn't no fire in this heat wave. People sweated, smoked and melted, but didn't catch fire.

I think it was a government conspiracy. In June of '69, some big defense contractor wanted to open a plant here. But folks didn't want it; picketed, protested, packed in monthly supervisors' meetin's. So this weapons maker packed up and left. But I have a theory. At a supervisors' meetin', where them defense contractors announced they was changin' their minds, some bigwig corporate lawyer said somethin' like, "We was just tryin' to create jobs and give you'se opportunities. We didn't expect this much heat." Interestin' enough, nothin' ever happened to none of them three supervisors, includin' Pop, who was chairman, and died of natural causes in 1999.

True, nothing happened to the rest of the population 'til two years later, but you know that sayin': revenge is a dish best served cold. Or in this case, hot.

# Keeping Your Head above Water

Immersed up to her neck in tepid water, Marisol had a thought that should have disturbed her greatly. What if she were to suddenly submerge, open her mouth wide and inhale deeply, allowing the surrounding liquid to fill her lungs? Why she was possessed of a morbid curiosity to experience drowning she didn't know. She was not depressed, nor given to such macabre whims. She imagined that she was alone on that sultry night in late August, in a place where the only sound of which she was aware was the soft humming above her. She could see neither sky nor clouds nor moon. Marisol fell into a trance, her head and the knuckles of both hands protruding from the clear water.

*Maybe death's not so bad,* Marisol told herself. She recalled studying existentialism in a high school philosophy class. Life had no real meaning, leaving two logical choices: terminate this pointless embodiment, or give it a purpose. A deep breath. Then two or three more. Terminate this pointless embodiment, or give it a purpose. What purpose?

Marisol became aware of a slow spinning sensation through her body, as well as the feeling that someone else was present. The latter did not frighten her; she didn't feel the need to open her eyes. Whatever happened would happen. Human beings all had the gnawing desire to act on dangerous, even deadly, impulses. To jump from the top of a tall building, perhaps to experience falling through the air. To steer one's automobile into the path of an opposing truck. The rush. The thrill. The adrenalin. The end.

When Marisol was in fourth grade, she brought a doll to Show and Tell, a doll that ate, drank, cried and ... yes, that too. Living Lucy, she was called. A gift from Grandma Susie. But Devin McGannon and Charlie Shupe killed Living Lucy, accosting her and Marisol on the playground after school and twisting her plastic head until it snapped off. Lucy had emitted a final, eerie wail in her artificial death throes. But this was not enough for Devin and Charlie, who then threw the hapless, headless toy to the ground and stomped her repeatedly, punctuating each stomp with a diabolical yell. Laughing, the pair of miscreants had left Marisol standing on the bleak, cold concrete, sobbing and clutching her decapitated doll. But that was long ago.

Terminate this pointless embodiment. The initial sensation had transformed from a strange caprice to a strong urge. *No*, Marisol insisted, *I'm not sad. Life is not tragic, but it's superfluous.*

The water, as well as the ambient temperature, seemed colder, although still not uncomfortable. An aura of happiness had descended upon her, happiness which seemed to emanate from another source, yet embedded itself in Marisol's consciousness. Breathe in, breathe out.

But the happiness was tainted, almost like the gloating of a scolded sibling who succeeds in getting an older brother or sister disciplined. She imagined that the same kind of "happiness" seeped surreptitiously into drunks and drug addicts lounging in dank alleys, and waiting for death.

Would it actually work? There was only one way to find out. All that Marisol had to do was lower her head, open her mouth ...

With a horrified start, Marisol grabbed the porcelain edge of the bathtub and hauled herself to a sitting position. Panting hard, she pulled the drain stopper out of the basin, listening to the potentially-deadly water being sucked down the drain. Then she remembered. Marisol wasn't superstitious, and had thought nothing when she heard that the previous tenant had drowned right there, where Marisol was taking a bath. There was no note, but the large amount of sleeping pills and alcohol found in her system left no doubt as to her intention. The tub was empty. Marisol distinctly heard the humming of the overhead fan, much louder than before. The temperature in the bathroom had returned to normal. Shivering in spite of this, Marisol stood up, stepped onto the waiting bath rug, and grabbed a towel. *Some spirits haunt subtly,* she thought, running the dry towel over her naked body, which was now bristling with goose bumps.

# Just Because You're Paranoid

Prone to panic attacks since childhood, Dawcet Gring nearly had an episode when he walked into the chiropractor's office for the first time. Some nagging feeling told him that Dr. Josh Campbell had evil intentions. Of course this was ridiculous, and Gring suppressed his fears and sat in the waiting room. He had to do something about his lower back spasms.

A lanky man in a lab coat came out to greet him, leading Gring to a door at the end of a short hallway. "Dr. Josh," as he insisted on being called, instructed Gring to sit in a wooden chair next to a chiropractor's table. The doctor grabbed hold of the sides of Gring's head and twisted his neck sharply. Unbearable pain shot through the patient. He couldn't move his head. Or neck. Or anything. Dr. Josh smiled.

"Kathy, Emma," he called. "Come in here, please."

Two young aides dutifully trotted into the examination room. Both seemed calm.

"A perfect rupture of the vertebral artery! Patient is 'locked in!'"

The young women giggled with delight.

# The Bunk Bed Incident

Vladimir Moroz praised his luck at finding an abandoned cabin a few miles outside of Dawson City in the Yukon. The small wooden building was structurally sound, as comfortable as any similar edifice could be in the 30-below weather, and sufficiently isolated from the boisterous mining town. It presented Moroz with the opportunity to murder another of his fellow prospectors, Anatoly Litvenko.

Most of the would-be miners who flocked to the frigid recesses of northwestern Canada in 1897 had fared poorly, losing their fortunes in search of greater ones, and many, their lives. Moroz had been a successful trapper, but switched vocations when news of the glittering discovery at Bonanza Creek reached his ears. He convinced another trapper, Jacques L'Enfant, to accompany him, as well as two of Moroz's countrymen, Litvenko and Alexander Karpov. The latter had an unfortunate encounter with a Kodiak bear, who mauled Karpov to death after smelling the beef jerky that Moroz had stuffed in his slumbering comrade's coat pockets. Even if his plan had failed, Moroz could have claimed that Karpov had been too drunk to remember hoarding the food.

Now there was one fewer companion with whom to share. The considerable yield that the four had uncovered near El Dorado Creek had prompted them to pack up and head south towards the town of Dyea, where they would take a barge to Vancouver.

Moroz was a large man, and therefore surprised when Litvenko agreed to let him take the top bunk. L'Enfant bedded on an old cot. Quickly learning that his berth was unsteady, Moroz decided on a risky plan that, if successful, would eliminate a second partner and look like an accident.

****

An hour after the trio had extinguished the lantern, Moroz shifted his weight back and forth, stopping momentarily upon hearing a loud creak. He waited a few minutes before beginning again. A soft cracking came, then a tremendous snap. Moroz broke into a demonic smile as he plunged five feet and landed with a thunderous boom.

His smile vanished, replaced with a grimace. He heard padded footsteps. Litvenko and L'Enfant stood over him, the former holding the lit lantern. L'Enfant looked horrified; Litvenko, calm.

"I slept on the bearskin rug near the door," he explained to Moroz, who lay immobilized with a shattered spine. "My bunk was uncomfortable." He then added softly in Russian, "Sasha hated beef jerky."

# About the Contributors:

### Allan M. Heller:
Allan is the author of five non-fiction books, numerous short stories and dozens of poems. In February of 2014, he was appointed poet laureate of Hatboro, Pennsylvania. He resides with his dear wife, Tatiana, and their wonderful cat, Rocky.

### Stan Horwitz:
Stan has been an avid photographer for the past 42 years in his spare time. Stan works full time as an information technology specialist at Temple University and he lives with his cat Darwin in the Art Museum section of Philadelphia.

### Teresa Tunaley:
Originating from the UK but now residing in the Canary Islands, Teresa creates with her electronic tablet and pen in software such as Photoshop, Corel Draw and Paint Shop Pro. Her work can be seen online and in print across the UK, US, Canada, Denmark and Europe. Her website: http://teresatunaley.wix.com/artstopper.